EARLY BIRD STORIES™

Luis's First Day:
A Story about Courage

Mari Schuh   Illustrated by Natalia Moore

LERNER PUBLICATIONS ◆ MINNEAPOLIS

NOTE TO EDUCATORS

Find text recall questions at the end of each chapter. Critical-thinking and text feature questions are available on page 23. These help young readers learn to think critically about the topic by using the text, text features, and illustrations.

Lerner Publications Company
An imprint of Lerner Publishing Group, Inc.
241 First Avenue North
Minneapolis, MN 55401 USA

For reading levels and more information,
look up this title at www.lernerbooks.com.

Photos on p. 22 used with permission of: HappyKids/Getty Images (soccer); xavierarnau/Getty Images (talking with teacher).

Main body text set in Billy Infant. Typeface provided by SparkyType.

Library of Congress Cataloging-in-Publication Data

Names: Schuh, Mari C., 1975- author. | Moore, Natalia, 1986- illustrator.
Title: Luis's first day : a story about courage / Mari Schuh ; illustrated by Natalia Moore.
Description: Minneapolis : Lerner Publications, [2023] | Series: Building character (Early bird stories) | Includes bibliographical references and index. | Audience: Ages 4-9. | Audience: Grades 2-3. | Summary: Even though he is nervous on the first day of school, Luis makes new friends, participates in class, and learns that courage is key.
Identifiers: LCCN 2022010107 (print) | LCCN 2022010108 (ebook) | ISBN 9781728476346 (library binding) | ISBN 9781728478371 (paperback) | ISBN 9781728481753 (ebook)
Subjects: CYAC: Courage—Fiction. | Conduct of life—Fiction. | First day of school—Fiction. | Schools—Fiction. | LCGFT: Picture books.
Classification: LCC PZ7.1.S33655 Lu 2023 (print) | LCC PZ7.1.S33655 (ebook) | DDC [E]—dc23

LC record available at https://lccn.loc.gov/2022010107
LC ebook record available at https://lccn.loc.gov/2022010108

Manufactured in the United States of America
1-52215-50655-5/26/2022

TABLE OF CONTENTS

CHAPTER 1
SO VERY NERVOUS

Today is the first day of school!

My stomach feels funny.
I'm so nervous.

What if my teacher calls on me? What if everyone stares and laughs at me?

Dad gives me a hug at the bus stop. "Have courage, Luis, and you'll do great," he says.

Check! Why is Luis nervous?

CHAPTER 2

BEING BRAVE

The bus pulls up, and I get on. There's a boy sitting by himself. "Can I sit with you?" I ask.

I think I made
a new friend!

9

At school, I see lots of
new people.

I'm going to have courage, just like Dad said. I say hi to everyone.

11

Uh-oh, I don't remember where my classroom is! My stomach feels funny again.

Wait a minute . . . I can ask for help!

At recess, I see a girl playing alone.
She tells me her name is Kia.

"Want to play together?" I ask her.
"Let's join the big game!"

Check! How did
Luis make a friend
on the bus?

15

CHAPTER 3

FACING MY FEAR

Back in class, my teacher wants a student to lead a sing-along.

What if he asks me?

Then I remember I had courage today. I rode the bus, asked for help, and made new friends. I can do this too!

I take a deep breath and say,
"I'll lead the sing-along!"

19

Dad was right. I had courage, and today ended up being fun.

I think tomorrow will be fun too!

Check! What was one way Luis had courage?

LEARN ABOUT COURAGE

Everyone feels afraid sometimes.

Doing something new takes courage.

It takes courage to meet new people.

It takes courage to ask for help.

Having courage is doing something that's hard to do, even though you're afraid.

THINK ABOUT COURAGE:
CRITICAL-THINKING AND TEXT FEATURE QUESTIONS

When was a time when you had courage?

Who is this book's illustrator?

How can you help others have courage?

What page does chapter 1 start on?

LERNER
SOURCE

Expand learning beyond the printed book. Download free, complementary educational resources for this book from our website, www.lerneresource.com.

GLOSSARY

courage: the ability to bravely face hard tasks or situations

nervous: worried about something

sing-along: a fun time when people sing songs together

LEARN MORE

Dinmont, Kerry. *Afraid.* Mankato, MN: Child's World, 2019.

Johnson, Kristin. *Sophie Learns to Listen: A Story about Empathy.* Minneapolis: Lerner Publications, 2023.

KidsHealth: Feelings
https://kidshealth.org/en/kids/feeling/

INDEX